PRAISE FOR *MINGUS FINGERS*:

"In *Mingus Fingers*, David Sandner and
Jacob Weisman have given us a quietly
intricate and intelligent merger of boxing,
jazz music, the seductive lure of the artistic
impulse, and the ultimate meaning of it
all. I read it with pleasure and admiration.
Highly recommended."

—RICK WILBER, AUTHOR OF *ALIEN MORNING*

"A stroll through jazz, boxing, the creative
fire, and the prices of all three. Subtle,
profound, and moving."

—KIJ JOHNSON, AUTHOR OF *THE RIVER BANK*

"Scenes of jazz and boxing in 1950s San
Francisco are interrupted by unexplainable
transformations . . . the narrator plays with
Charles Mingus, during which the trumpeter
witnesses Mingus become a giraffe . . . the
odd magic and arresting imagery captures the
feel of jazz."

—*PUBLISHERS*

D1210982

BOOKS BY DAVID SANDNER

<u>Non-fiction</u>
*The Fantastic Sublime: Romanticism and
Transcendence in Nineteenth-century Children's
Fantasy Literature* (1996)
*Critical Discourses of the Fantastic,
1712-1831* (2011)

<u>As Editor</u>
Fantastic Literature: A Critical Reader (2004)
The Treasury of the Fantastic
(co-edited with Jacob Weisman, 2013)

BOOKS BY JACOB WEISMAN

<u>As Editor</u>
The Sword & Sorcery Anthology
(co-edited with David G. Hartwell, 2012)
The Treasury of the Fantastic
(co-edited with David Sandner, 2013)
*Invaders: 22 Stories From the Outer
Limits of Literature* (2016)
The New Voices of Fantasy
(co-edited with Peter S, Beagle, 2017)
The Unicorn Anthology
(co-edited with Peter S, Beagle, 2019)
The New Voices of Science Fiction
(co-edited with Hannu Rajaniemi, 2019)

MINGUS
FINGERS

[signatures]

MINGUS
FINGERS

DAVID
SANDNER
& JACOB
WEISMAN

FAIRWOOD PRESS
Bonney Lake, WA

MINGUS FINGERS
A Fairwood Press Book
Copyright © 2019
by David Sandner & Jacob Weisman

All Rights Reserved

No part of this book may be reproduced or transmitted
in any form or by any means, electronic or mechanical,
including photocopying, recording, or by any
information storage and retrieval system, without
permission in writing from the publisher.

Fairwood Press
21528 104th Street Ct E
Bonney Lake WA 98391

**See all our titles at:
www.fairwoodpress.com**

ISBN: 978-1-933846-87-3

Fairwood Press First Edition:
November 2019
— Also available in ebook

Cover image © Getty Images
Cover design by Patrick Swenson
& Elizabeth Story
Book design by Patrick Swenson

Printed in the United States of America

For George Clinton and Sun Ra,
celestial travelers.

SAT ON AN OLD, BATTERED plywood stool in the shed behind the house, playing trumpet along with Erskine Hawkins' new record, "Tuxedo Junction." One of the legs of the stool was too short; every time I tapped my foot, keeping time, the stool tapped counterpoint. I had gotten used to it.

My sister's son, Kenny, ran about the yard chasing rabbits. A copse of trees abutted the backyard. Beyond the trees lay a warren, a large pile of rocks, or a small hill, mazed with burrows. There must have been fifty, maybe a hundred rabbits back there. I had long ago given up gardening, or even trying to fence them out, and had learned to ignore them—the easy hopping always at the edge of my vision, the sudden scattering when I came upon them unawares. Kenny had been trying to catch one all afternoon. He would creep up in front of one, trying not to startle it. The rabbit would lift its head from the grass, watch Kenny until he got too close, then bolt to safety through the copse of trees. Kenny would follow, but not nearly quick enough. I should have found the whole thing impossibly funny, but Kenny looked too much like my sister to make anything funny. He had her wide-set eyes and high cheekbones. I missed her. I'd tried to get her to move up to San Francisco with me, to get away from that husband of hers, but that hadn't worked.

I'd had only had Kenny for about two weeks, ever since my sister's house had burned down in Los Angeles. Martha was staying with our mother back in Louisiana until things got settled with the insurance company. Meanwhile, Mom had asked me to look after Kenny. She didn't like Richard any more than I did and wasn't about to put up with him in her house. She'd taken Kenny's older brother, Lamond, but she'd felt Kenny needed to grow up with a real man around the house. I would have to do. Kenny seemed like a good kid, although a bit on the quiet side. He was only six, and things were tough for him right now. Just the other night I'd caught him crying in bed after lights out. I didn't know what to say to him. I didn't know if I'd ever get the hang of this father thing. And already it had made the music thing that much harder. I wished I could have said no to my mother. My life, a jazz musician's life, barely brought in enough money for me, and it wasn't a very good life for a kid. But it took too much effort to refuse. "Only for a little while," my mother had said.

Kenny was getting tired now, and sweat was running down his cheeks as he dashed about the yard. He sat down in the middle of the yard. The rabbits, as always, emerged from the trees to eat the grass whenever Kenny was still, inviting him to try to chase them again.

Distracted, I trailed off my own playing and listened to Hawkins' record, nodding along, the stool tapping a beat. Like a lot of material I'd played over the years, it was rhythm and blues disguised in a jazz idiom. Nice, but not very difficult. The trick came in Hawkins' mellow groove and soft tones; the ease with which he played that was difficult to emulate. I had to get up to turn the record over on the turntable, so Kenny surprised me when he spoke. He had come up beside me.

"Someone here to see you," he said.

I looked at him. He had a rabbit cradled in his arms. How had he done that? For a moment, I thought Kenny wanted me to speak to the rabbit. Then I wondered if Kenny should be holding it. It was a wild animal, if only a rabbit. But before I could speak, a man stood at my door. Kenny had backed away, and stood outside petting the rabbit and watching the man warily. And for good reason: a white man who'd evidently squeezed through the hole in the fence of our front yard after not finding anybody home was quite an anomaly.

The man took off his hat and extended his hand. I placed my trumpet back in its case. I hadn't put the needle down on the record yet, and just let the turntable slowly spin. The man introduced himself as Karl Radcliff.

"You've been a hard man to find," he said grinning. It was a grin that came easy to him, and meant exactly nothing. He seemed friendly enough for the moment, but I didn't trust him. I'd seen his kind before, both working in jazz clubs and in my former profession, boxing. I could tell by his damaged nose and fingers he was here about the boxing.

"I was down at your gym a couple of days ago, but nobody had seen you in months."

I waited for him to continue, but he seemed to want some sort of explanation.

"I don't fight anymore, Mr. Radcliff," I told him.

"I hope that's not true," he said. He grinned wider. "I saw your last fight, against

Bratton. You gave him a real battle."

I remembered the fight all right. I didn't think anybody had ever hit me so hard before, punches I'd have expected from a heavyweight, crushing blows that splintered my ribs and left me seeing double for months after the fight. Certainly not the punches of a welterweight. As I'd circled around him, trying to stay out of reach of his jab, not wanting to let him hurt me again with another combination, I realized for the first time that there was a another level to the sport that I had never before encountered. Within two years, in 1951, Bratton would win the National Boxing Association title by beating the Italian, Charley Fusari, in a fifteen round decision. But I didn't know that then.

"He was a tough one," I said. "What can I do for you?"

"I represent Kid Galvistan," he told me handing me a card that I put in my wallet. "You stood up to Bratton so well, we figure you'd be a good test for the Kid, see how good he really is."

I knew of Kid Galvistan, and nobody needed to see how good he really was. The champ wouldn't fight him, and nobody else wanted to either. Bratton had been strong, but his big baby face and a gentle smile let you know that none of the damage he was inflicting on you was personal. By contrast, the Kid was a monster. He was a bulldog who wouldn't stop pounding away at your body until you got tired and dropped your head. Then he'd go for the kill with a vicious uppercut. No way did I want a piece of him, but the potential pay day made it tempting. I looked out the door for Kenny, but he and the rabbit were gone.

"I'll give you a call if I change my mind," I told him. "I'd need to start training again. When would you need an answer?"

After I'd let him through the house and out the front door, I sat down in the living room, trying to think of a way I could make the same amount of money by not fighting. The music paid a little, in fits and spurts, but not as much as a steady gig with a championship contender. And if I did well and the Kid didn't put me in the hospital, I would probably also get another good paying fight after that. I knew enough already to know that there was no way I could expect to win the fight. One more fight, I told myself, just to get through the summer. Then I can retire. Again.

I went to the kitchen and got myself some lemonade. I stood drinking the lemonade from the pitcher before the open door of the refrigerator. I thought about calling Liza to see what she would think. I knew what she would say; she'd be worried about me, but she'd also be excited about the money. Perhaps I just wanted someone to talk me into taking the fight. I felt I needed to stop worrying about myself so much and just do what I knew I had to do. When I went to the phone, I remembered Kenny out back, and the Hawkins record still spinning in the shed.

I looked out the kitchen window and saw Kenny sitting cross-legged in the middle of the yard, surrounded by rabbits, one in his lap, another putting two paws on his chest to sniff at his face, a dozen others all around. Butterflies flew in and out of the trees this time of the year, and they had come into the yard in numbers, thirty or forty, and fluttered close around Kenny's head. What the hell? I stood dumbfounded. What was with this kid? What was I getting into? Suddenly, I laughed, loud and long.

THE NIGHTHAWK WAS A DUMP. IT was old, dank, and smelled of beer and cigarettes. The tables were tiny and surrounded by too many chairs. It was a wonder that the patrons could find room to fit their drinks on the tables. But somehow the summer fog that washed through San Francisco every night muted all the dirt and grime until all that was left was the music. I loved the place.

I sat on stage waiting to play, trumpet lowered, but still pressed to my lips. Kenny sat at the back of the club with Liza. They had a special section for underage patrons, a fenced off area way in the back that made you feel that you were watching an exhibit at the zoo rather than a live performance by human beings. Liza hated sitting back there. Kenny loved the Nighthawk. Maybe he just wanted to get closer to me, but if so, it worked. I took him there most every night I played, and many other nights as well, enough nights that I began to feel guilty about it. He'd made friends with Helen, the owner's wife who worked the cash register at the front door. She'd let Kenny eat or drink anything he wanted and wouldn't charge us a thing. And watching Kenny happy, bobbing his head along with the music, slapping the beat on a table top, was a relief from the Kenny I had to live with the rest of the time. He was so quiet that I'd almost forget that he was there and then he'd turn up all of a sudden, right under foot. The club brought us both relief. But I'd decided I'd make an effort to be a real parent, and keeping Kenny up late at night seemed to be one of the things I was going to have to stop doing. Just not tonight.

Tonight, the after hours session was really cooking. If it hadn't happened to me before, I don't know what I would have done. Instead when the bass players' appearance began to change, I merely squinted my eyes in an effort to pretend everything was normal. It wasn't, though. The groove he was laying down was too smooth, too pure. I even knew enough to expect the change when the music was that good. His skin began to blotch and his neck began to stretch until I was looking at a giraffe in a tuxedo. Nobody else noticed; nobody else ever did.

The first time it had happened I was just out of high school, playing in a band back in New Orleans in a club on the corner of Eighth and Franklin. Two other bands were waiting to play and were about to move us off when our Creole piano player, Isidore Washington, began banging on the keys. It was a sound of jubilation, unlike anything I'd ever heard. When I looked up at him he wore a sickly smile and looked for all the world like a hyena.

We played the rest of the evening. Nobody was going to move us off that night.

Only a few months ago a local group, the Dave Brubeck trio, had made a name for themselves at the Nighthawk, recorded a couple of albums and moved on. Now there was a new group fronting the club. Red Norvo, the xylophone player who had made some recordings with Benny Goodman, had his own trio featuring Tal Farlow on guitar and Charles Mingus, the giraffe, on bass. I had heard about him, but none of it did him justice.

Norvo and Farlow were fine players, but Mingus was fascinating, his deft long hands gliding effortlessly across the strings. His eyes would scrunch tightly and his face would twist into a grimace as if he were frustrated that he couldn't shut out the world and just be left alone to play his music without the benefit of an audience or backing musicians. Mingus had played with everybody I admired: Louis Armstrong, Dinah Washington, Lionel Hampton, and Duke Ellington, staying only long enough for a cup of coffee with each one before moving on. In the end, though, he must have been too defiant, too much his own man. Tonight? Well, tonight was something special. He'd surpassed himself and altered himself in a way I didn't quite understand. What would it feel like, I wondered, to play at that level? When I'd fought Bratton, he'd had something of that intensity, too. But he hadn't changed. If he had, he probably would have killed me. Only the music brought the change.

Mingus—the giraffe—opened his eyes. He looked out at the club, then straight at me. I realized I hadn't played a note yet. I had been mesmerized by his playing. I thought he was going to yell at me about it, but he just nodded toward the back of the club.

"That's your boy, isn't it?" he said loud enough for me to hear.

I looked out at Kenny, not quite understanding the question. *My boy?* It didn't seem quite right.

"My son? No," I said. "My sister . . ."

Mingus dropped right back into playing. He turned away from me. And then,
impossibly, he took his playing up to a
whole other level. One maybe I didn't
know existed. One I didn't want to know
existed. The giraffe tilted his long head
back and began to croon, his neck undulat-
ing at the effort. The weird keening thrilled
me like an electric shock, a shiver running
up my spine. I started to play. Smooth and
deep. This was what it was all about. Not
those endless nights out on the road. Not
the endless hours practicing, hoping to be
able to record a record nobody would ever
listen to anyway. None of that mattered,
just to be in the moment. I never changed,
though. I waited for it, but it never came.

After the show, when everybody else
had gone home, Mingus sat at the piano on
the stage, Kenny standing beside him looking up into his face while Mingus played,
explaining how chords went together, how
the music went together to make music out
of noise.

Mingus was a man again, a young man with a sharp, hurt look in his eyes. He leaned back and half-turned to me as I came up. He put one hand on Kenny's shoulder.

"You have to teach him to play," Mingus told me.

I nodded. "He likes Count Basie, a lot," I said. "He's crazy about Billie Holiday and Louis Jordan."

"He knows the good stuff already, now he just needs to know the bad. Then he can play in the soul." I wasn't sure what Mingus was talking about anymore, but I nodded anyway as if it all made perfect sense. "He's got to know the agents and their cut, the club owners and their cut, the people never letting you be, the women." He leered when he said *women*. "Then he can play just for himself, and everything will come out like morning dew—like the first day."

Kenny looked at me as if asking my permission. Did he want to become a jazz player? My mother would never forgive me.

"Is that what you want?" Mingus asked him.

Mingus didn't slur like a drunk, but there was a rambling quality, a headiness to his speaking that made him seem distracted, even as he stood right in front of you and looked you in the eye.

"We've got to go, Mingus."

"You come back to play, tomorrow."

"I'll be here." But I wasn't sure that I would. The vision of Mingus as a giraffe, the impossible music, and his ramblings had left me a bit unnerved now that the thrill of playing had passed.

"And bring the kid. Teach him so he learns right. All that bad stuff, he'll learn on his own. You teach him the good stuff. You teach him the underground."

I nodded. I already knew that was Mingus's language for the place he went when the music was everything and he didn't have to think at all, the underground. Every musician called it something.

Kenny and I hardly spoke on the way home. In truth, I didn't know what to say.

"So," I felt like asking, "do you want to be a trumpet player like your uncle?" But Kenny had fallen asleep on the back seat.

I dropped Liza off at her mother's where she lived. I hadn't invited her over since Kenny's arrival. She didn't like that any better than having to sit at the back of the club behind the fence. As I thought, she had liked the fight idea, though. I think she thought I was better than I was—than I would ever be. She kissed me quick and got out without a word. I couldn't blame her. I didn't have much to offer her lately. She was twenty-two, working in a shirt factory. She lived for the nights at the club, for dressing up in tight dresses, listening to the music, and talking to the musicians. I was losing her fast. And I couldn't blame her at all. I watched her walk up the step, unlock her door and go inside without looking back.

I had to carry Kenny up to his room when we arrived home. When I turned to leave the room, I caught Kenny looking at me in the mirror on his dresser. When I turned back at the doorway, he had closed his eyes again and pretended to be asleep.

I heard a tap at the window. A butterfly outside fluttered against the pane. Soon there were two, then five, tapping softly like light rain. Kenny pretended not to hear. Later, when I checked on him on the way the bathroom, I found the window open and seven or eight butterflies nestled around Kenny as he lay curled up on his side. In the morning, they were gone.

THE FIRST PUNCH HIT ME LIKE A sledge hammer, pushing through my jaw, trying to get into my head. I shook it off and approached my sparring partner from the left, trying to keep him off me with a series of quick jabs. I hadn't boxed in what seemed like ages and it was coming back to me slowly. Not the timing, but the drive and willingness to absorb the pain.

I took another shot, this time in the ribs, that took all the air out of my stomach. I was going to have to get much sharper if I was going to box again, lose fifteen pounds or so. The foot speed just wasn't there yet.

I got in close and grabbed the back of his shoulder with my glove, clinching him in tight, not letting him throw another punch until I'd gained back my wind. I hit him on the arms a few times with a combination that didn't do any damage, but gave me a chance to back away.

Hal, my trainer, rang the bell. He looked up at me from the floor below ringside and just shook his head.

"What are you doing in there?" I didn't want to talk to him. All I wanted to do was sit down, curl up in a ball and go to sleep for a million years.

"Too slow?" I asked.

"Too slow, too stiff, too stupid." It was Hal's job to inspire me.

"I'll be okay."

"Sure you will. Come back tomorrow and we'll work on it some more."

"Two more rounds," I pleaded.

"If you get hurt now, I don't get paid. Come back tomorrow."

WARMING UP THAT NIGHT, I HAD trouble blowing my trumpet. My lips hurt and the whole left side of my face felt heavy. I had a nice shiner starting to form. The other musicians kept their distance, nodding at me knowingly, wondering what back street alley I'd stepped into.

My trumpet was flat and so was my spirit. Kenny was eating what looked like two or three slices of pizza at his table, listening to music, but looking a little preoccupied. He hadn't liked it when I'd come back home with my face looking like raw sausage. He'd insisted on touching the side of my face and running his hand along the long, sinewy bruise that ran from my eye down to my jaw. It had taken all of my strength not to flinch.

"You're paying your dues." Mingus. I looked up. "That's cool. Really."

"Mingus . . ."

"No, I mean it. You're a fighter, right? A what-do-you-call-it, pugilist?"

"I don't . . ."

"Larry over there," Mingus motioned behind him with the back of his thumb, "he washes cars. In the summertime he's out there everyday without his shirt on over on Columbus, washing away. Tony, the light skinned clarinetist, he once fronted a klezmer band. Barney drives a cab, maybe he'll even give you a lift home one of these nights." I didn't question Mingus on how he knew any of this. Sometimes he seemed oblivious, as if there was nothing but his music. Other times, he seemed to know everything about everyone.

"Me, I've played in every big band you could name. I play a backbeat all night long, every night. Maybe I get a solo or two when nobody's listening. I might as well be playing that rhythm and blues crap. Might as well play in some lounge or at one of those bar-mitzvahs. It pays the rent, don't it? Then we can come out here and jam. Only you're selling a bit more of yourself than the rest of us, one piece at a time. A nose here, a shoulder there. Tonight it was your lip. You got to be ready to give it up before it takes the one thing you got, before you lose your chops for good. Then every night will be tonight."

I started to say something, I wasn't sure what, but he just put his hand up.

"You'll know when the time is right. Something will let you know."

Nobody likes being called a whore. But when you're called a whore and told that it's okay to be one, it leaves you angry but also a little ashamed. It took a lot of nerve, though, for Mingus to say something like that to someone like me, someone who he knew could do a lot of damage when he wasn't made to wear a pair of gloves. I struggled for an answer, the blood rushed to my head and into my injured cheek, where it burned, throbbing in rhythm with my pulse.

Mingus left before I could form any sort of reply.

"Kenny," I heard him call as he passed by me.

"Charlie!" Kenny ran up to Mingus.
Charlie?

Mingus caught him with both hands

under Kenny's armpits and lifted him in the air.

"You had spots and a long neck," Kenny said, as Mingus lifted him onto a wide shoulder. "You had a large spot right here." Kenny drew a circle around the side of Mingus's neck.

This couldn't be happening. Nobody ever saw any of it but me.

Mingus nodded. "When you get underground, it'll happen to you."

I sat dumbfounded. I didn't get a chance to talk to Mingus before we started playing. Once during the set, Mingus just laughed at me, at the expression I couldn't wipe off my face. Shock. That's what it's like when a private madness becomes something casually spoken about by others. Impossible. My world had "mother-may-I" taken two giant steps to the left.

Right in the middle of the set, Mingus leaned in to me and whispered something I couldn't quite hear.

Then he turned away. Mingus knew all about it. Maybe that would change everything, help me understand. And Kenny? Before the set finished, all hell broke loose.

I saw the gun flash, even in the smoke. Chairs pushed back, some people screamed, more cried out "gun!" People crouched down. An argument in one corner had turned ugly, five or six men standing, bumping chests, becoming a brawl, then the gun waved. It didn't even fire. I jumped off the stage and headed for Kenny. Some guy, not even involved in the fight, tried to jump me. He didn't last long. I hoped I didn't break his jaw, but I didn't have time to take it easy. When I got to Kenny, Liza had him by the hand and was crouching behind a table. He looked wide-eyed, but calm, quiet. He knew not to be conspicuous when trouble started.

I moved Kenny and Liza up by the stage, rules be damned. I was glad I did. After a few minutes, we tried to play again. But the mood in the Nighthawk had turned bad. People milled about, eyeing each other, waiting for trouble, cursing, knocking bottles to the floor or pushing at one another. Then there was gun fire outside—two shots. Then order through a bull horn. The police had gotten involved. No one wanted that. In a colored neighborhood, at night, nobody wanted that. The place cleared out, people pushing out like they had all done something wrong. Like being at the scene was a crime itself.

I left with Mingus, Liza, Kenny and the other musicians out the stage door. We stuck together, piling in Barney's large Ford, Kenny on my lap and Liza squeezed in beside me, and he drove us to our own cars in turn.

Later we learned, in the same way we got all our news, through word of mouth, that the guy the police had shot out front wasn't even involved in the fight inside. He was standing out by the curb, drunk, in the wrong place when trouble was happening. He wasn't armed. They shot him twice.

The next night, I was back playing music, but I left Kenny at home. And Mingus had taken the night off. Everything sounded off and I hadn't any heart for it.

RED NORVO'S GIG AT THE NIGHT-
hawk ended the following week,
and he and Mingus moved on. Kenny
asked me about Mingus a couple of times
and I didn't know what to tell him. Finally,
I told him Mingus had gone away for a
while, but in all honesty I had no idea if
he'd ever be back this way again. People
were always coming and going from my
life.

I STARTED TRAINING AGAIN THAT
week, running a route that took
me through the Fillmore and Mission
Districts and then up to the top of Potrero
Hill. I'd use my last reserve of energy to
sprint up the dirt roads until I got to the
top and you could see the bedrock jutting
out of the earth. I'd find a spot in the sun
overlooking the bay and sit and eat my
lunch, fending away the goats. Some days,
when I didn't feel like going home and
practicing my music, I'd walk down to

the water and follow the piers along the Embarcadero, stroll through the Presidio, and walk out to the ocean before making my way home.

It was hard that first week. I'd gotten soft around the middle and I could feel my lungs burning for air even as I started out. But as time went on it got easier.

CIRCLED AROUND MY OPPONENT, JAB-bing, keeping him at arm's distance. My sparring partner this afternoon was Lawrence D'Antoni, a burly Italian bruiser who'd once had a shot at the title but had more recently gone to seed. Fat rippled his middle and he had a hard time breathing as he moved about the ring. He was still dangerous, though. One blow and I could easily wind up on the canvas, wondering what day of the week it was.

All of the fighters Hal hired to help me train were big men with quick hands and a knock out punch, like the Kid. Many of them belonged in higher weight classifications, all of them had reach on me, some by as much as half a foot. If I was going to be prepared for Kid Galvaston, I'd need to be ready for the punishment his long, spindly arms could deliver.

D'Antoni was being patient, not rushing in to get inside my jab. Slowly he crept after me, closing ground. If I let him get me into a corner, as washed up as D'Antoni was, I might not get out before he'd done enough damage to keep my ears ringing for a few days. I wanted him to come inside, to duck my jab and leave himself wide open. So far he wasn't taking the bait.

I circled back the other way. D'Antoni threw a jab of his own. When I pushed it aside, he threw a right that I could hear as it parted the air beside my head. I ducked. Standing up, I threw everything I had into an uppercut to the body. The smack was deafening, but D'Antoni seemed unfazed. At last the bell rang.

Hal ran up, wiped my face with a rag and gave me some water. My arms ached and my feet were blistered from all the running, but it was hard not to smile. I still wasn't fluid, my thinking in the ring a bit mechanical, but I'd come a long way in just a few weeks. For the first time, I began to suspect I might have something for the Kid after all.

I was playing a set at the Tin Angel when I next ran into Mingus. The Tin Angel was a converted warehouse on the waterfront that was cluttered with all kinds of trinkets that the Angel's owner, Peggy Tolk Watkins, had collected. She called them found objects.

They played mostly Dixieland at the Angel. Not usually my cup of tea, but Kid Ory was fronting a band there and I wouldn't have missed it for the world. When I was a kid, growing up in New Orleans in the Garden district, I'd see Ory all the time, carrying his big trombone case late at night, rushing off to work. I'd snuck into his backyard once to hear him practice. Ory had always had the best trumpet players in his band, and to play alongside him, now that I was older, was as close to being Louis Armstrong as I would ever get.

Dixieland can sound mechanical when it's played by people who've only heard it on record, but tonight we had a good group and the music was swinging hard. It all seemed to be led by a bouncing baseline. I turned around to see who was playing bass and Mingus winked at me.

"How's Kenny," he asked me when we'd finished. "I hoped he'd be here." He hoped *Kenny* would be here?

I thought about trying to explain to Mingus that I was just being a good parent, but the whole situation was just too absurd. Had Mingus really known that I would be here? I didn't believe it, maybe deep down, maybe, but not on the surface where I expected everything to make sense.

"I'm going south, to Los Angeles. I'll be back through in a month. I wasn't planning on it, but I will now."

I nodded. Kenny had something. I

hadn't heard him play anything, but I knew. Mingus knew it, too. I never would. And it was clear that more would be open to him, things I didn't know about, couldn't even dream of.

All you had to do was look around. Jackie Robinson, Roy Campanella, Monte Irvin, Willie Mays and a host of other black baseball players were tearing up the big leagues. It was only a matter of time before the same thing happened and our music came crashing through the ghetto that had held it for so long.

I was a good jazz player. I was a good boxer supporting myself as a musician. But I wasn't great. I didn't have it. Kenny did.

I BOUGHT KENNY A SET OF BONGO drums the next day. They were cheap and it seemed as good a place to start as any.

His face lit up when he saw the drums and he hugged me hard around the knees. I promised myself I wouldn't push Kenny, that a jazz musician's life shouldn't be pushed on anybody. But the joyous glint in his eye when he saw the drums for the first time shattered my resolve and I knew I would do whatever it took to help him on his way.

I STAYED INSIDE ALL DAY MAKING love to Liza. I didn't have many more chances. She seemed to know it, too. Our lives were drifting apart, and there just wasn't much to hold us together. Afterwards, we smoked a cigarette between us, lounging on the bed, enjoying whatever time was left. I had fifteen years on her. She enjoyed things the way they had been. I could understand that. But something had to change for me. Whether I liked it or not, I could feel it coming.

Kenny was out back, tapping on his bongos. He wasn't too bad, for a kid, and Liza and I joked about how long it would be before he could sit in with me. When the tapping finally stopped, I thought I'd

better check on him. He'd been out there
alone for hours. I left Liza the cigarette
and pulled my shirt on, leaving it unbut-
toned over my white undershirt. I slipped
my shoes on without bothering with socks.

I found Kenny out by the rabbit
warren, surrounded, as usual, by a crowd
of rabbits, lazily hopping and chewing
grass. The butterflies were there again,
too, circling his head and landing on his
shoulders. Even some birds seemed to have
hopped to the branches closest to Kenny.
It didn't look strange anymore. Funny how
you could get used to things.

"Who are you, Dr. Dolittle?" I laughed.
Only Kenny seemed able to make me
laugh lately.

Kenny had turned his bongos over and
was dropping dirt inside. Not the way you
treat your instrument, but I had just left
him alone for hours and was feeling guilty
about it, so I let it go.

"I don't want you to fight," he said.

Kenny didn't even look up at me. He
had grass stains on his white and orange

striped shirt and on his jeans. I knelt down beside him. The rabbits hardly moved, hopping languidly. Guess they'd gotten used to me, too. I could have touched one. I could have had it for dinner.

"I already promised," I said. I knew Kenny didn't like the injuries I came home with, but this was the first time he'd said anything so blankly. "You know," I said, "too many of your friends are rabbits. You need to get back with your brother, have some kids your own age around."

Kenny nodded. "I know. Not yet," he said. "Soon." What did *that* mean? Kenny looked at me with his wide brown eyes. "I have to see Charlie again."

Have to? Kenny could be so matter of fact that it was disconcerting, even when he was loading dirt in his bongos like any other kid. Why did he have to see Mingus? I was almost afraid to ask, somehow. Mingus wanted to see him, too, though I didn't say that. Jealous, maybe.

"He'll be around soon," I said. "Maybe after the fight."

"You might get hurt bad this time."

"I can take care of myself."

"No, this is different."

Again so certain of things, so serious.

"How do you know that?"

"Charlie."

What was this? Was Mingus scaring Kenny? I was starting to get angry.

Kenny just looked at me. That egged me on in some way.

"Look," I told him. "I'm your uncle. Mingus has no right to scare you like that." Even as I said it, I knew it was something more. I could see it in Kenny's face. He wasn't talking about boxing this time, he meant the next fight in particular.

"It could be really bad this time."

What had I gotten myself into? How could Kenny be so certain of things? More than whatever it was Kenny had, more than knowing that Kenny would probably make the change someday, would know what that felt like, I envied him his certainty. I had drifted into music, into boxing and out again. How could he know things so young? Had I known once and forgotten?

I wandered inside. Liza was in the kitchen, her long flowered dress buttoned wrong, rummaging in the refrigerator.

"How's Kenny?"

"He's fine."

No, I was the one in trouble. I could feel something cold in the pit of my stomach. I had no idea what was coming. But no more drifting. I was going to face it head on.

I WAS BACK IN THE SHED, FOOLING around with a riff I'd come up with from listening to an old Jimmie Lunceford recording, when Mingus showed up next. The record had long since run out, but I left it spinning and the static emanating from the speakers made my playing sound as if it were a recording.

"That's nice," Mingus said. Kenny sat in the crook of Mingus' arm. "I heard a little Clark Terry in there, too. Nice."

Mingus had his bass held steady in his other hand. He put Kenny down. "Let's play," he said.

I wanted to be angry with Mingus. I didn't have much time left to train for the fight. It had been nice to just relax and play, but I didn't have time for much more. I laid the trumpet aside, wiping it with a rag and putting it back in its case.

"Mingus," I said. "Why don't we go into the house. Can I get you something to drink?" It was a hot day for San Francisco. There were few clouds in the sky and the sun had managed to hold the fog at bay for several days.

As we crossed the yard, Kenny's hand in Mingus', a crowd of rabbits followed at a respectable distance.

"Hippity-hop, man," Mingus said, turning to Kenny and making a face. Kenny laughed. Mingus was in a good mood, soaking up the sun and radiating it out. Even I was starting to feel better, starting to realize just how tense I'd been lately.

I grabbed a couple of beers from the icebox, handed one to Mingus and introduced him to Liza, who shook his hand. I gave the other beer to Liza and poured two glasses of water from the faucet for Kenny and me. Kenny, back in the doorway, looked doubtful about his place among so many adults until Mingus waved him in.

Mingus looked about the room until he found Kenny's bongos on the floor by the couch. He motioned to Kenny. *Yours?* Kenny nodded. "Want to play something for me?" Mingus asked.

Kenny looked at me, unsure. I was about to say something, tell Kenny he didn't have to if he didn't want to.

"Come on," Mingus said, turning to me, "let's show the kid what we've got. Let's go play something."

I shrugged. Why not? Mingus was not to be denied, not today.

It was crowded in the shed with Mingus and Kenny. I had to unplug the turntable and push the stool back against the wall. Liza came out to watch and stood in the doorway. She had to shy away from the butterflies that also waited in the doorway.

"The bass," Mingus told Kenny, "is a lot like playing drums. A really good drummer is judged not on the music he plays but on how much better he can make the other musicians."

Mingus started us off with a couple of slow blues numbers from the Mississippi Delta. Mingus would play the part of the guitar, very simple, very sparse. I'd play the vocals on my trumpet. Soft, pleading numbers.

Each note Mingus played reverberated as strings snapped against wood, eschewing virtuosity in favor of raw emotion. We played this way for a while, my trumpet echoing the voices of Muddy Waters, Elmore James, Brownie McGee, and Mississippi John Hurt. Every once in a while I'd strike a more modern lick and Mingus would make a face. "That sounds like Art Farmer," he'd say. "Where did Dizzy Gillespie come from?" Mingus squinted his eyes and looked around the room.

Mingus was goading me to play in a style of my own. Over the years I'd gotten comfortable borrowing a phrase here and another phrase there, relying on a common language to express an idea. Mingus wouldn't let me do that. At first I felt restrained playing this way. As we began to play more modern compositions, though, I began to see what Mingus was after.

Playing with Mingus was certainly more challenging than anything I was used to, like walking a tightrope without a safety net. I was used to imitating other musicians to make a wry comment about the music, but this was special, joyful, if I didn't fall flat on my face.

But I didn't. I found myself playing better than I ever expected I could play. The notes just seemed to happen. I'd think a thought and the sound would come out effortlessly, as if my lips and hands were extensions of the sound and not the other way around.

Mingus spoke while he played, leading me onward, saying "That's it" over and over, almost to himself but to me, too. Or, with a wry chuckle, "What's that you have to say?"

I knew Mingus was pushing me to my limits, knew that if we went any farther, or if I thought about what I was doing too much, I'd falter and wouldn't be able to continue.

A sweat broke out all over my body, making me run hot and cold, flushed and then shivering with excitement. I must have closed my eyes because when I opened them the room was darker, as if a cloud had covered the sun. But that wasn't it. *Underground*, I thought. But that wasn't it either. I was startled, but I stayed with the music. Mingus was still there. Kenny was there, his head down, bowed into his bongos, playing, staying with the beat as if he couldn't stop. It kind of scared me to see his intensity. What he played was simple, but pure. How did he do that?

My heart felt steady but beat way too strong, pounding against my chest. I

glanced out the doorway of the shed trying to see what had happened to the light.
Was I going blind?

The doorway wasn't there. We weren't
in the shed.

As my eyes adjusted, I saw there were
windows looking out out on a moonlight
bayou. It was night here. I had seen swamp
like that only in Louisiana where my fam-
ily, and Kenny's father, came from. Maybe
it was somewhere else, though. Maybe it
was nowhere at all. Had Mingus created
it all, or been drawn to it?

I looked at Mingus. He had changed,
his impossibly spotted neck bent almost
to breaking as he loomed over us, his long
face noble and calm.

Mingus moved his hooves along the
strings, shaking his long head in time. Had
I changed? I couldn't tell. I looked down
at myself and I didn't seem any different.

The shed's four walls seemed to close
in on us from a long way away. The world
seem to unravel in a spiral, as if Mingus
was putting all the toys he'd taken out to

play with back in a box, one by one. Liza clapped as we finished, my horn sounding one long last wail. I hadn't seen if Kenny had changed. But I knew he would someday. And I never would. Mingus had taken me there.

Mingus leaned forward.

"Now you know," he said. And I knew the whole show had been for Kenny, not me.

Mingus walked over to Kenny and tousled his hair. "I've got to go and I don't know when I'll be back. But now you know the way."

I was surprised to find it was evening outside. There was a cool breeze blowing in from the ocean, thin wisps of fog floating through the back yard. How much time had passed? It didn't seem that we had played so long. Kenny was exhausted and went right to sleep as soon as Mingus left.

That night Liza and I made love, the window open and the cold air touching us whenever we parted. After, I laid back holding her, smoking, staring at the ceiling, thinking about what happened in the shed. Would it be enough to have been there once? I wasn't going to get to go back. I felt that to be true. Some only see through the doors others will walk through on their way somewhere else. I had a lot to think about, a lot to try to unravel about the music and what I had heard and what it meant. It was more than most. It was enough. It had to be.

T HE FIGHT WAS AT HARRY FINE'S Gym in Oakland. The fight might have been a high profile fight, at least for me, but we were still a long way from Yankee Stadium or Madison Square Garden where Joe Louis often fought. Hell, it wasn't even the Civic Center Auditorium in San Francisco.

But it was home. Most of my early fights had been there as the undercard to bigger fights. Pasted along the dark mahogany wall panels, hundreds upon hundreds of posters, all displaying earnest fist-cocked men, promoted countless fights from bygone eras. A few of them, no doubt, bore my name.

The bout before mine ended in a split decision and my name was announced. I slapped my gloves together to get my blood moving and walked out of the dressing room. My adrenaline caught with the restrained roar of the crowd and I jogged into the ring.

Bratton, the man who had beaten me into an early retirement, stepped over to my corner to wish me luck. I acknowledged him by tapping my glove to my forehead.

There was a loud rumble among the stands. Kid Galvistan stepped out of the other locker room and walked slowly down toward the ring as if he didn't have a care in the world, as if he was mildly annoyed that he'd had to show up.

Young fighters climbing into the ring often appear dazed, even a bit glassy-eyed. The handshake is the social event before the rumble. The referee will grab you and tell you how he wants a clean fight.

Your opponent may even wish you luck. Galvistan seemed completely at ease.

His face wasn't pretty. It was long and drawn and riddled with acne scars below the neck. His hair was cut close to the top of his head, leaving only a thin layer of kinky hair. But his arms were what drew my attention. They were amazingly long and powerful. If he held them at his side and did a squat, they would touch the floor.

I was still wondering how I'd be able get inside of his long reach without getting clobbered myself when we touched gloves.

Galviston sneered as he came out of his corner. He closed in quickly. I hit him with a jab and moved quickly to my right. I didn't want to stay in one place too long. We circled around each other a couple of times. He jabbed and I ducked and the blow sailed harmlessly over my head. Then he caught me with an uppercut, a glancing blow along my temple.

My vision blackened around the edges and a chill swept through my body. He followed with a savage combination. I felt, rather than saw, three blows land across my body. Two somewhat low on my chest and another, that sucked my breath away, on my side. A fourth just missed my face, the sweat—my sweat—flying off his gloves and spattering my cheek.

Time to wake up.

Galvistan came at me again. I threw another jab. Galviston parried it easily with his right, momentarily exposing his chin. I was too far away, though, to do anything about the opening. It was clear he didn't think I could touch him if he didn't want me to. Not with those long arms.

I threw another jab just to be sure. Again, I could see his chin. Then the bell rung.

I sat down heavily. Hal wiped my face off with a towel and poked me a bit to make sure I was all right. He was silent and methodical in his treatment.

I took another blow to the head in the third round and two more in the fourth. I was able to shake them off, retreat, and regroup, a little wobbly but intact. As long as I stayed conservative I'd survive the fight, but I was falling behind on points. If I lost another couple of rounds my only chance of winning would be to knock him out.

Coming out of my corner to start the fifth round, Galviston caught me with a jab that smacked off my forehead. The crowd roared as Galviston charged in, punching with both hands and driving me back to the ropes. I managed, somehow, to keep both hands up in front of me and caught most of his punches on my arms and gloves. Galviston paused, slowed his assault, and then paused again. I pushed him back toward the center of the ring with two hands.

Galviston started forward again. I caught him with a jab, jabbed again. He deflected the second jab, once more exposing his chin. This time I leaped forward and caught him with a short right hook which snapped his head back in a spray of sweat. I followed with a left uppercut which drove him back several steps.

The crowd roared.

I pressed on. I could see his eyes getting real small and his balance begin to falter. Inside his reach, I drove a combination to his body. He stumbled back to the ropes. I chased after him, caught him flush with a left to the chin, then several more shots to the body. Then I felt his weight on my back as he grabbed me and held me tight. He was so strong that I couldn't move.

Galvistan held on until the referee came in to break us up. I circled cautiously around him as he tried to keep me away with a series of jabs, using his long arms to keep me out of reach. The bell rang.

I was tired. I'd taken a lot of punches and thrown much of what I had into the last round. Still, Galviston seemed to be worse off. A cut had begun to form along the bridge of his nose and there were bloodstains on his shorts.

Hal slapped me hard on the back and poured water over my brow. He was beginning to feel that maybe, just maybe, I could win this fight.

I had abandoned everything we'd worked on in practice. I'd stood toe to toe with the Kid and slugged it out and I was still standing.

Maybe, I thought, as the bell rung to start the sixth round, maybe boxing wasn't that different than music. I'd always been a good boxer but never a great one. In the same way, I'd never been a great trumpet player. But I'd reached something special inside myself playing with Mingus out in the shed. I'd abandoned my set phrases and gone out on my own. Perhaps I could do the same thing as a boxer.

Galvistan crept in cautiously. I could see by the way his right arm bobbled that he was looking for my jab. I jabbed anyway. Galvistan covered up, no longer exposing his chin. I threw a punch that must have looked as if I were swinging at his chin. Instead, I waited for him to raise his glove and put everything I had into a blow that landed squarely on the inside of his right shoulder. Maybe I could take some of the punch out of him that way at least.

Galviston's face contorted in rage. Tiny drops of blood stood out along his white mouthpiece. He moved in, caught me with a jab, and threw a wild combination that was a flurry of motion but left me unscathed. When he was finished, I popped him on the shoulder again.

I was feeling good now. My nerves were calm and my motion fluid. I shuffled my feet as Galvistan came after me again. I felt like a well-oiled car easing into third gear. I'd never felt this comfortable in the ring.

Everything he did seemed to be in slow motion. I could read what he was about to do by the way the muscles flexed along his forearms or by the way he clenched his jaw or furled his brow. I could see it all before it happened. After every series of punches he threw, I'd hit him with a single clean, solid blow, either on his shoulder or where I'd opened a cut on his forehead the round before.

Nothing had ever been so easy.

Then I felt the change. The muscles on

my back pulled out, unfolded. The hair on arms and back began to thicken. Feathers? Wings? I looked down at my hands, expecting to see large talons, but saw only boxing gloves. Dark, black feathers lined my arms.

Galvistan must have hit me then, because suddenly the canvas reared up and struck my face. Then blackness.

I LEFT FOR EUROPE NOT LONG AFTER the fight. I stayed for a few months until my mother called Kenny home to reunite him with his brother. I told Liza I was going on tour. I never came back. I stayed in Paris awhile, where the people loved jazz, and mostly my color didn't matter. I went to London and Berlin, just passing through. A lot of bombed-out buildings remained from the war, but new ones were going up everywhere. Sometimes the people seemed a bit dazed, frantic to make things better after looking down into a dark, dark place. They replaced the past a building at a time.

After a while, I didn't want to be on the beaten track anymore. I went down into Spain and fell in love with its bright and open countrysides. The civil war had ended badly, but it didn't have any effect on me. I found a small village away from everything else. I married a local woman who thought I knew some secret of life from America that I embedded in my music. I thought she was like sweet wine. I wanted to hold and savor her, slowly, a lifetime's worth.

I toured sometimes, sitting in with whomever came through from the U.S. circuit. It was enough. I thought a lot about the change and the music, the meaning of it like poetry, but I never could have said what it meant to me. I thought about Mingus and Kenny from time to time. I never saw Mingus again, and didn't see Kenny for a long time. I didn't envy Kenny anymore. I knew his ability would take him far beyond anywhere I ever went, but I was at peace. You can ask for more, I suppose. I certainly had. But I learned better. Mingus would spend time in an asylum after the death of his friend Eric Dolphy. He stopped playing for a few years after that, but he eventually reemerged on the scene, beginning a second career as a composer. And Kenny, when he did come through and see me, years later, touring with his own band, well, the living hadn't been easy for him either. We didn't talk about Mingus, hardly talked at all. Kenny seemed to be somewhere else most of the time. Of the three of us, Mingus, Kenny and me, I thought I was the lucky one.

ABOUT THE AUTHORS

DAVID SANDNER is a member of SFWA and the HWA. His work has appeared in *Asimov's*, *Weird Tales*, *Realms of Fantasy*, *Pulphouse*, *Mythic Delirium*, and anthologies *Baseball Fantastic*, *The Mammoth Book of Black Magic*, and *Tails of Wonder and Imagination*. He is the author of *The Fantastic Sublime* and Mythopoeic Award-nominated *Critical Discourses of the Fantastic, 1712-1831*, and editor of *Fantastic Literature: A Critical Reader and The Treasury of the Fantastic* (with Jacob Weisman). Edited collection *Philip K. Dick, Here and Now* is forthcoming. He is a Professor of Romanticism and Popular Literature at California State University, Fullerton.

JACOB WEISMAN is the publisher at Tachyon Publications, which he founded in 1995. He is a World Fantasy Award winner for the anthology *The New Voices of Fantasy*, which he co-edited with Peter S. Beagle, and is the series editor of Tachyon's critically acclaimed novella line, including the Hugo Award–winning *The Emperor's Soul*, by Brandon Sanderson, and the Nebula and Shirley Jackson award–winning *We Are All Completely Fine*, by Daryl Gregory. His writing has appeared in *The Nation*, *Realms of Fantasy*, the *Louisville Courier-Journal*, *The Seattle Weekly*, and *The Cooper Point Journal*.

Photo © 2018 by Michael Arnzen

OTHER TITLES IN THE
NOVELETTE SERIES
from Fairwood Press:

The Specific Gravity of Grief
by Jay Lake
small paperback: $8.99
ISBN: 978-1-933846-57-6

Welcome to Hell
by Tom Piccirilli
small paperback: $8.00
ISBN: 978-1-933846-83-5

If Dragon's Mass Eve Be Cold and Clear
by Ken Scholes
small paperback: $8.99
ISBN: 978-1-933846-86-6

Slightly Ruby
by Patrick Swenson
small paperback: $8.00
ISBN: 978-1-933846-64-4

ALSO FROM
Fairwood Press:

All Worlds are Real: Short Fictions
by Susan Palwick
trade paper $17.99
ISBN: 978-1-933846-84-2

The Arcana of Maps and Other Stories
by Jessica Reisman
trade paper $17.99
ISBN: 978-1-933846-91-0

Truer Love and Other Lies
by Edd Vick
trade paper $17.99
978-1-933846-85-9

The City and the Cygnets
by Michael Bishop
trade paper $19.99
ISBN: 978-1-933846-78-1

The Girls With Kaleidoscope Eyes
by Howard V. Hendrix
trade paper $17.99
ISBN: 978-1-933846-77-4

Street
by Jack Cady
trade paper $17.99
ISBN: 978-1-933846-90-3

The End of All Our Exploring
by F. Brett Cox
trade paper: $17.99
ISBN: 978-1-933846-71-2

The Sacerdotal Owl
by Michael Bishop
trade paper: $17.99
ISBN: 978-1-933846-72-9

*Seven Wonders of a
Once and Future World*
by Caroline M. Yoachim
trade paper: $17.99
ISBN: 978-1-933846-55-2

Paranormal Bromance
by Carrie Vaughn
Signed & numbered hardcover: $35.00
ISBN: 978-1-933846-73-6

On the Eyeball Floor
by Tina Connolly
trade paper: $17.99
ISBN: 978-1-933846-56-9

**80+ More Titles Available at:
www.fairwoodpress.com**